2009

Gold Mountain Girl

By Katherine Blanc

INFINITY
PUBLISHING.COM

Copyright © 2009 by Katherine Blanc

ISBN 0-7414-5510-2

Published by:

INFINITY
PUBLISHING.COM

1094 New DeHaven Street, Suite 100
West Conshohocken, PA 19428-2713
Info@buybooksontheweb.com
www.buybooksontheweb.com
Toll-free (877) BUY BOOK
Local Phone (610) 941-9999
Fax (610) 941-9959

Printed in the United States of America

Published July 2009

For Alexis Rivera

Gold Mountain Girl

CONTENTS

Author's Note

The year is 1901, and California's last gold rush is quickly coming to an end. 13 year-old Callie Rose Miller is on a mission: To free her family once-and-for-all from the grip of "gold fever" and get back to their farm in Bakersfield, where they belong.

Callie endures harsh living in Gold Mountain City in the San Bernardino Mountains––a boomtown that's going bust. Thanks to new friends and a beloved schoolteacher, she and her brother Charles manage to make the most of their stay. But all the while, Callie is hoping for that one big chance to break away from this land of broken dreams.

The opportunity finally arrives. Now Callie must convince her father that the *real* gold he seeks is waiting for them back home.

Chapter 1: *Mama Would Never Approve*

"This town is worse than the last one," Callie Miller declared as the family wagon rolled into Gold Mountain City. She was tired and sore and her mouth was gritty with dirt. They bumped along a row of rickety wood buildings, passing a saloon, a blacksmith shop, a barbershop, and a general store. Callie scratched her head and wondered if every town south of Bakersfield looked exactly the same.

The wagon jerked to a halt in front of the store. Pa jumped down, rubbed his back, and tied up the horses. "Come on," he grumbled as he walked through the swinging door.

1

Charles nudged his big sister. "*You* go first," he said.

"No, *you* first," she replied. Her brother had insisted on playing this silly game for months; whoever went first was the loser. Callie wasn't about to let him win yet another round. Her bottom ached from the hard wooden seat, but she refused to budge an inch.

Pa poked his head out the door. "Get in here, both of ya!" he hollered. As they dropped from the wagon, Callie listened for the crunch of Charles' boot touching the ground.

"Ha-ha, you're first!" she teased him. After four dreadful days on the trail, she savored this small victory.

Day turned into near night as they entered the store. Shafts of light beamed through the dim structure, catching shimmering particles of dust.

A pinch-faced clerk leaned over the worn counter. "What can I get ya?" he asked.

Pa pulled a piece of paper from his pants pocket. "Let's see...I need bailin' wire, matches, rags, a sack of flour, jerky, soap flakes, and some firewood...and one of them gold pans."

The clerk eyed him sideways, and Callie heard men chuckling in the back of the store.

"What's so funny?" Pa asked.

"Nothin'," the clerk replied coldly. He pushed his way through the aisles, tossing provisions into three canvas sacks. Then he plunked the sacks onto the counter top. "That'll be $3.50," he said, not bothering to look up. Pa laid a few silver coins on the counter. They each grabbed a sack and headed for the door. On the way out, Callie sensed several pairs of scowling eyes beating on their backs. They'd just arrived here and already she felt unwelcome.

The wagon jostled out of town along a dirt road lined with tiny ramshackle cabins. Callie spotted three large white houses further up the hill, and for a moment she was hopeful. But as the wagon slowed down in front of the cabins, her heart grew heavy.

"Which one's ours, Pa?" Callie asked, afraid of his answer.

"Which one did ya want, Honey?" He gave her a wink.

"None of 'em." Not one of those cabins looked suitable for a home. Instead they resembled big sheds—— the kind that hold rotting, forgotten things. She shook off a chill as the strong March wind gusted up slope, blowing dust into circles that swirled around them.

Pa eased the horses to a stop and pointed at the most rundown cabin on the road. "Well, I guess this here's our home sweet home," he said.

"*This* one?" Callie's voice cracked from the dry air. "Tell me you're joking." The cabin slumped to one side, tired and forlorn. Its front door was ajar as if someone had rushed out of there. In all of her 13 years she'd never seen such a shameful little shack.

"A rat wouldn't live in a place like that," Callie mumbled under her breath. She closed her eyes, hoping it was all just a bad dream. But when she opened them, everything was still there, unfortunately.

Charles leaped from the wagon and ran toward the front of the cabin. He jumped onto the porch and turned to Callie. "Come down!" he yelled, waving a skinny arm.

As she stepped onto the porch, a musty draft of air billowed under her skirt and lingered around her leggings.

"*You* go inside first," Charles said with a daring smirk.

Callie backed off of the creaking timbers. "There's no way I'm going in there till Pa says it's safe." This wasn't a game anymore; she was genuinely scared.

Pa cleared his throat. "Are ya two gonna' stand there all day? Help me out over here." He stood at the back of the wagon steadying a wooden crate.

"Easy now, Callie," Pa cautioned as he loaded the crate onto her back. "Ya got your Mama's thin build. Don't want ya to break nothin'."

Callie was proud to have her mother's fine-boned frame; she also had her strong will.

"Mama would've never put up with this," she protested under the weight of the crate as she staggered to the porch.

Charles was a small 10 year-old, but in his mind he was the size of Paul Bunyan.

"Here Pa," he said, "You can load me up double." Soon his little body was piled high––a snail wearing an oversized shell. "I think I can make it if...if..."

CRASH! Charles came down in a tumble of tin cans, followed by a jumble of cuss words.

Pa ran his fingers through his scruffy beard. "Awright," he muttered, "From now on I'll take 'em inside and you empty 'em." The wind banged the cabin door against its frame.

"Please make sure it's safe in there first," Callie pleaded.

They followed Pa into the one-room cabin, brushing cobwebs from their faces.

"See, this ain't so bad," Pa said. "And look at all the stuff they left us." Dishes sat on the kitchen counter, pots and pans were stacked in an open cupboard, and a wooden table stood at one end of the cabin with three stools tucked underneath. In the center of the room was an iron cooking/heating stove with a pile of firewood beside it. The place looked as if someone had left in a hurry, which made Callie immediately suspicious.

Charles waited in the doorway as Pa slid another load inside. This was their mother's wooden travel trunk, which Callie had insisted on bringing along. So far, they had lugged it to three mining towns in the past five months. Charles shoved the heavy trunk across the gritty floor with his foot.

"Be careful with Mama!" Callie cried.

Charles narrowed his brown eyes at her. "Will you please stop calling this old thing 'Mama'?" he scolded. "It's just some of her stuff in there."

"But it's all we have left of her," Callie shot back. Last autumn, tuberculosis had caught their mother's very soul, whisking it away like a cyclone. She refused to let Mama's memory fade into nothingness.

Callie dropped to her knees and tugged on the trunk lid, which stubbornly yawned open. The sweet scent of lavender poured out, veiling Callie in comfort. Thankfully Mama's treasures were safe: the bible, the wedding dress, the unfinished quilt, and the dreaded corset. But where was the choker? The one she'd wanted to wear for years? Callie dug deeper until soft velvet greeted her fingertips. She unrolled the tight bundle of fabric, hoping it held the precious piece of jewelry.

"The choker!" She heaved a sigh of relief and clicked open the locket and smiled at the small photograph tucked inside. There they were, Mama and her two babies captured forever in a happy moment. Callie snapped the locket shut and fastened the choker around her neck.

Three worn-out canvas cots sagged in a corner of the room. Charles wobbled across the room, straining under the weight of another crate.

"Which bed is yours?" he asked.

Truly, not one of those rat-knawed things was worthy of being called a *bed*, but Callie certainly didn't want to freeze to death, so she picked the one closest to the stove. By the looks of that saggy smelly cot, Callie figured that someone must've let his horse sleep on it. Charles dropped the crate onto the canvas, raising a puff of brown dust.

Pa appeared at the door. "I'm takin' the horses up to the corral," he said. "See if ya can get some supper goin'."

Callie was about to open the old stove, but...what might be lurking inside it? She held up a matchstick, feeling like a helpless little girl.

"Please light the stove for me Charles," she begged, "Just this first time." Charles swung open the heavy door, tossed in an armload of wood, and sparked a fire on the first try. Soon the cabin glowed cozy-warm.

Callie turned back to the crates scattered willy-nilly on the floor. "Hmm, if only I could find the skillet..."

Suddenly there was a knock at the door. Who could *that* be? It certainly wasn't Pa. She tiptoed to the door and put an ear to the wood.

Charles pressed himself flat against the wall with an ax raised over his head.

"Who's there!" he demanded, using his deepest-possible voice.

"It's Mrs. Metzger, your neighbor," a woman replied. "We live in that first white house up the road there. I saw you pulling in earlier and figured you could use a hot meal."

Open the door, Charles motioned. Callie cracked it open slightly, peering around its edge. A pale, plump woman stood on the porch. Her thick arms were wrapped around a large pot. Pointy-toed boots projected from the bottom of her wool skirt.

"I'm sorry we can't offer you folks something finer," she said, " But the supply wagon only comes to town once a week and, well...this is the best we could do." She held out the pot.

Callie hesitated, but her growling stomach instructed her otherwise. "Oh, you really shouldn't have. Thank you Ma'am." As she reached for the pot, a savory aroma escaped from it. Charles called off his attack and stood at Callie's side.

"Why, hello there young man," Mrs. Metzger said as her round blue eyes scanned the cluttered room. "Where's your Ma and Pa?"

"Pa's at the corral," Charles said, "and Mama's..." he looked at the trunk and then at Callie "Um...Mama's gone to be with the Lord."

Mrs. Metzger's eyes lowered and her puffy cheeks drooped. "Rest her soul...well, uh, please enjoy the food. And do give our regards to your Pa." She edged backwards off the porch. "And remember, school starts tomorrow. The new schoolhouse is up the road just past our house. You'll hear the school bell ring just before 8 o'clock."

How wonderful it was to have hot food ready to eat! Callie had never been treated so kindly by a stranger; perhaps she'd judged this town too harshly. As she car-

9

ried the pot to the kitchen table, she promised herself that she'd return Mrs. Metzger's favor.

Charles lifted the lid and put his face over the pot. "Chicken stew!"

"Be careful, silly boy," Callie warned, "The steam is hot enough to burn your eyes."

Pa dragged himself through the front door and kicked off his boots.

"You're just in time," Charles said as Callie set three bowls on the table.

As he approached the kitchen table, Pa noticed the pot. "Now wait a minute," he said as he sat down, "How'd ya come up with this?" Charles looked over at Callie and she put a finger to her lips. This would be their little secret.

As the three of them slurped their hot stew, Pa eyed Callie.

"I don't recall no chicken in our wagon," he said, poking a spoon around in his bowl. "And I don't recall no potatoes neither."

Callie and Charles looked straight ahead, pretending they couldn't hear him.

"Well?" Pa stopped eating and stared at them through his bushy eyebrows.

Charles snickered and watched his feet. Callie figured that Pa must've been wearing a puzzled expression and she didn't want to see it. She jumped up and cleared the table.

"I'm glad you liked your supper Pa," she said, hurrying the bowls over to the washtub. Maybe if she kept busy with the dishes long enough he would stop asking about the stew. At last, Pa got up from the table and went over to his cot. Callie smiled at Charles; their secret was safe.

Darkness shrouded the sky outside the windows. Pa lit an oil lamp, which bathed the cabin in a dim orange light. The three of them got to work arranging their cots and preparing for bed. Callie scanned the cabin for a place to change into her night clothes. When she was younger she had never cared much about privacy, but now that she was 13 it mattered. There was nothing to hide behind; she'd have to change underneath a blanket. She was about to grab one when she spied a wooden screen folded in the corner. It was perfect. Callie unfolded the screen and placed it behind her cot.

"This area is for ladies only," she announced, claiming her turf.

Once they'd settled into their cots Pa turned down the lamp. The cabin was now pitch black inside; Callie waved a hand in front of her face and couldn't see a thing. To make matters worse, she had a head full of pesky thoughts that whirled around her like a swarm of bees. Wide awake, she propped herself up on one elbow.

"Pa," she called out in the dark, "I'm worried about school tomorrow."

Pa let out a tired sigh. "Ya ain't got nothin' to worry about," he assured her, "Yer brother will be there with ya. Come on, get some sleep."

Callie tried to sleep, but her head was bursting with more and more thoughts until they spilled from her mouth.

"I hate being the new girl at school...I hope we have a nice teacher...Goodness, I haven't been to any kind of school in months...What if I've unlearned all of my learning?" The words continued to pour out. "I wonder how our farm is doing...Do you think Uncle Joseph will harvest the alfalfa on time?...And what about the animals?"

"Go to sleep! *Right now!*" Pa bellowed. Callie pulled the covers over her head. This was going to be a long night.

Chapter 2: *Ready or Not*

The next morning Callie sat with Charles and Pa at the kitchen table, wrapped in a blanket. Her eyes were puffy and her ears still rang from the piercing howls of coyotes that had circled the cabin all night long.

They silently ate their cold cereal, which made the morning seem even colder. Callie pulled the blanket snugly around her shoulders.

"I'm sorry about this breakfast, Pa," she said, "I'll have to figure out how to cook on top of that old stove."

Pa nodded toward the pot on the counter. "What about the stew ya made last night?"

Callie lowered her eyes. Dang! She'd slipped up.

"Hmm," Pa said, stroking his beard. "So someone brung it over here, eh?"

Charles couldn't hold his tongue a minute more. "It was the neighbor lady," he said.

Pa turned back to Callie and winked. "Ya see? This town ain't so bad, huh?"

Callie glared across the table at Charles. Who's side was he on anyways?

Pa checked his pocket watch. "Well, I'm headin' off to that stamp mill up at the gold mine. Gonna' try and get me a job." He looked around the cluttered cabin. "Where's my darn hat? I can't find a thing in this mess."

Charles didn't know if Pa was serious or fooling around. "Um...it's on your head."

Pa reached up and touched the wide brim of his felt hat. "Thanks son. Now you two get to school on time, ya hear?" As he closed the door behind him, Callie spun around and faced her brother.

"The *stamp mill!*" she yelled, stomping her foot on the creaky floor. "Pa talked about it the whole ride up here––as if it was a wonder of the world. But the truth is, it's nothing but a factory that crushes rocks. We'll waste our time here just like we did in the last three mining towns."

Charles didn't want to give up hope just yet. "Pa says the mountain's full of gold," he replied sheepishly, "and this time he swears that he'll strike it rich."

Callie folded her arms. "If Pa truly wants to strike it rich, why doesn't he get into a business that actually makes money?" She could tell by the looks of this town; he'd have no better luck here than he did at the other mines.

Charles rested his forehead on the table. "I know," he agreed. "I guess...well I guess I was just hopin' that things would be different this time." He looked sadder than a snowflake in hot sunlight. Callie sat beside her brother, cradling his face in her hands.

"I promise you that I'll find a way to get us back home to Bakersfield."

Charles' face brightened. "Really? Are we goin' back?"

Callie nodded, quite pleased with herself. "Now let's get ready for school, shall we?" She watched the brightness vanish from his eyes.

Callie crouched before the washbasin and held up a small mirror and squinted her eyes. "What a fright," she groaned. "My face is absolutely caked with dust." She rocked the basin back and forth. "Oh no," she gasped, "The water's frozen." In desperation, she grabbed a kitchen knife and picked at the slick surface. Bit by bit the ice chipped away until a small trickle of water spouted forth. She gratefully dipped a rag into the basin and wiped her face. But when she held up the mirror, she almost fell backwards.

"Good Heavens!" she shrieked, "Now I look like a mud pie!" There was no time to warm the basin on the stove, so Callie gave up worrying about it––what was the use? Besides, she was sure that children in this town were used to being filthy. She ducked behind her privacy screen in the corner and pulled on a pair of leggings, a heavy wool skirt, a sweater, and her thick fur hat.

Meanwhile, Charles wandered around the cabin in his underwear.

"I can't find my other boot," he whined. "How am I gonna' walk to school like this?"

Callie peeked around the screen. "You can wear a pair of mine if you want," she taunted. She finished dressing, then rummaged through the crate beside his cot.

"Here," she ordered, "Put these on. And quit fussing like a baby."

But Charles wasn't ready to quit. "No, not my *riding* boots," he complained.

Callie sighed at his supposed helplessness. "Do you have a better alternative? I swear it Charles Miller, you will be the end of me."

Just then, a bell clanged in the distance. Callie felt a knot tightening in her stomach. "It's time for school? Already?" she asked, hearing her voice tremble a bit. She hastily braided her hair while she scurried through the kitchen, stuffing a sack with dried fruit and jerky. Suddenly she stopped. "Where are the writing slates?"

Charles stood by the door, shrouded in gloom. His sweater was on backwards and his pants were unbuttoned. He shrugged.

"We *have to* find the slates," Callie insisted. She was not about to get in trouble on her first day of school. They would find those slates if it took all morning.

"Wait," Charles said, lunging toward his cot. He crawled under it; soon an explosion of clothing, tools, and toys came flying out. "Eureka!" he yelled, emerging with slates and pencils. Callie crammed them into the heavy sack. "Let's go," she said.

As she opened the cabin door, a small group of laughing, chatting schoolchildren passed in front of their cabin. Callie and Charles jumped from the porch and hurried to join the parade.

Chapter 3: *First Class*

The brand new one-room Gold Mountain schoolhouse was nothing much to look at, Callie thought as they approached. It was tiny just like their cabin, and thrown together from odd pieces of multi-colored scraps of wood.

A slim auburn-haired woman stood on the front porch swinging a bell that was mounted to a post on the porch. "Welcome to school," she said in a singsong voice.

"What is *she* so chipper about?" Charles sniped as they entered. "I'll bet she wouldn't be if she'd tripped over all those dang rocks tryin' to get here."

Inside there were eight desks set in two rows. Each desk was a different size; Callie figured they'd probably come from another school. The teacher's desk sat at the front of the room, and behind it were maps on the walls with a movable blackboard to one side. A bookcase leaned against the far wall alongside a faded American flag. One desk sat next to the heating stove. *At least I'll be warm*, Callie thought, dropping into the seat.

Charles slid into the very last desk in the very back. "Time for a nice nap," he said, plopping his head down on the desktop.

There were seven children in the room, three girls and four boys. Once everyone was settled, the teacher closed the schoolhouse door. Callie watched as the last bit of sunlight disappeared, replaced by the dull glow of a hanging kerosene lantern.

"Good morning!" the teacher beamed from the front of the room. "I'm Miss Margaret Oliver, and I want you to know that I feel privileged to be here. And you should also feel honored to be the very first class of pupils in Gold Mountain's history." She picked up her pointing stick and strolled to the back of the room and stopped next to Charles.

Miss Oliver tapped on his desk with her pointer and he popped his head up. "I must warn you," she said, "this desk was made from an old outhouse."

The children giggled.

"What's that supposed to mean, Ma'am?" Charles asked.

"It means that you probably shouldn't rest your face on it," she replied.

The class erupted into laughter, with Charles laughing the loudest. Miss Oliver had hit him squarely on the funny bone.

Miss Oliver glided to the front of the room and stood before the world map on the wall.

"Let's start with a lesson in geography. Can anyone tell me where England is?"

The room was quiet. Callie wasn't sure enough to raise her hand, and obviously no one else was either. At last Miss Oliver gave up. "It's right over here," she said, pointing.

Callie was glad she hadn't tried to answer that question. *Her* idea of England had ended up closer to Africa.

Miss Oliver went on. "Did you know that Queen Victoria ruled England for 63 years until her death in January?"

Ah, Queen Victoria! Callie'd had difficulty understanding the Queen's many ridiculous fashion rules.

Perhaps now they would change; this was her chance to find out. She raised a hand.

Miss Oliver looked relieved. "Please introduce yourself," she said, smiling.

Callie's throat felt dry and her face flushed slightly. "I'm Callie Miller, Ma'am."

"And what is your question, Callie."

"I don't mean any disrespect Ma'am, but...now that the Queen is gone, can ladies stop wearing their corsets?"

Miss Oliver awkwardly tugged at her own tightly-cinched waist. "Uh...I, I suppose that decision would be up to each lady individually," she replied.

The other children gasped at Callie's boldness. "Well then," she continued, "I've decided right here and now that I'll *never* squeeze my ribcage into a corset." Poor Mama had worn one of those awful things, Callie recalled, and she was always complaining about her sore back. Plus it had made it hard for her to breathe.

Callie looked at her teacher sympathetically. "Miss Oliver, I hope you'll reconsider your corset too because now that that silly old queen is dead, you no longer have to wear one." She was certain that her teacher appreciated the thoughtful suggestion.

Miss Oliver furrowed her brow and cleared her throat. "Children, it's time for a bit of fresh air. Let's take a short recess break." She'd have to watch that sharp-tongued Callie Miller, and do a better job controlling this new class.

The children filed through the schoolhouse door. Charles dashed out as if his trousers were on fire. He and the boys immediately dropped to the ground for a game of marbles.

Callie was the last one outside. She stood on the schoolhouse steps, feeling bored and a bit foolish. Further out in the schoolyard she saw two girls milling around a tree and holding the ends of a lifeless jump rope. The taller girl motioned to Callie. "We need one more," she called out.

Not wanting to appear rude, Callie skipped over to join them.

The tall girl spoke again. "I'm Bertha Metzger, and this is Martha Scham." Bertha had a large, rounded body, and Callie guessed she was maybe 15. Martha, on the other hand, was around 12 years old, thin and wiry with hair cropped short like a boy's. Her movements were jerky and rabbit-like.

"Let's jump!" Martha cried, tapping her feet on the ground.

Bertha calmly ignored Martha. "My mama brought you the chicken stew last night," she said, "I hope it was good."

Callie saw the resemblance between mother and daughter. "Oh yes we loved it, thank you. And I'll get your cooking pot back to you right away."

Martha had no patience for the small talk. "We usually make one of the boys hold the rope, but they turn it too fast," she said, in her rapid-fire way. "I'm so excited that we finally have three girls! You can jump first."

Callie tried to remember some of her favorite old jumping rhymes, but for some reason only one came to mind. "Let's do *Coffee & Tea*," she said with a shrug.

Bertha held an end of the rope while Martha held the other. Slowly it began to swoosh. Callie ducked into its spinning arc, carefully lifting her long skirt. With each turn of the rope the girls chanted together:

> I like coffee
> I like tea
> I like the boys
> And the boys like me.
> Yes
> No
> Maybe so
> Yes
> No
> Maybe so . . .

Callie's head began to feel lighter than a balloon. Her feet barely cleared the ground, causing her to trip. "Stop!" she pleaded, "Please stop!" The girls let the rope go limp. They watched in disbelief as Callie leaned against the tree, panting like a dog. "Don't worry," she said breathlessly, "I'll be fine. It's just that...whew...I'm not used to...the mountain air."

Bertha and Martha didn't seem to mind waiting, but Callie was tired of being stared at. Her school day had been humiliating enough already. "Here," she offered, "Let me turn the rope for you." She grabbed one end and Bertha took the other.

"What rhyme do you wanna' do?" Bertha asked Martha.

"None," replied the scrawny little thing, "I just wanna' jump, jump, jump!" As Martha hopped and bounced, Callie struggled to keep from laughing at this frog of a girl.

At last the school bell rang. As they headed toward the door, Callie decided that she'd best lay low for the rest of the school day. She followed the two girls, dragging her feet and wishing she could just go home.

Chapter 4: *The Bear Necessities*

Sometimes a week can drag like a feather through molasses.

As she wrestled with the breakfast dishes, Callie felt a frown spread across her face. Her mind wandered backward over the past few days. What was it about the new school that made her so unhappy? Well, for starters there really weren't enough children. Nothing was wrong with Bertha or Martha––or the boys for that matter––but with such a tiny group of friends in a tiny town like this one, every detail of her life was exposed, naked. Although Bakersfield was a small town too, it seemed to have more...space.

And then there was the matter of Miss Oliver. Callie had been disciplined by that teacher three times in one week for asking *important* questions, she believed. Now she'd have to make her big mouth smaller just to fit in around here.

Pa sat at the table oiling his work boots, while Charles wandered around the cabin looking for something he'd lost, as usual.

Suddenly there was a loud ruckus outside. Callie heard frantic shouts, the clatter of footsteps and the ping of pounding metal.

Pa jumped up and ran to the window and pushed the curtain aside, joined by Callie and Charles. "Why, there's a bear out there!" Pa exclaimed, "Looks like a grizzly to me." He opened the window a crack to get a better view. The massive bear roamed from cabin to cabin digging through trash piles and firewood stacks. Close behind was a circle of men yelling and banging on pots and pans.

Charles wrinkled his nose at Pa. "Why are they doin' that?" he asked.

Pa laughed. "It's supposed to scare away the bear," he said, "but it don't seem to be workin' too well." The beast went about its business unfettered.

A wild-eyed man dashed up to their window. "Stay inside! Bar the door!" he hollered.

Pa patted Callie's shoulder. "Now don'tcha worry one bit about gettin' to school," he assured, "I'm sure the critter will be long gone after while."

As Callie got dressed, the racket outside grew even louder. She doubted they'd have school today, which was certainly fine with her.

Pa checked his pocket watch. "Well, it's a half-past eight and that bear is still out there," he said, shaking his head. "I ain't heard the school bell ring and I ain't heard no work whistle blow neither. I'd say we're all stuck."

Charles did a little dance across the room. "No school! No school!" he chanted. Callie resisted the urge to join him in celebration.

The giddiness was halted by a thunderous roar. Callie bolted to the window.

"Psst. Pa," she nearly whispered, "Come look, there's more than one bear." Five grizzlies now stood shoulder to shoulder, combing the area in search of food.

Charles shoved his sister aside and pressed his nose to the glass. "Why, them bears are like a pack of outlaws!" he cried. They watched the outnumbered men scramble for cover.

"Ya know what them fellas shoulda' done," Pa said, "They shoulda' opened up the saloon and let them bears drink their fill. Then they coulda' just loaded the groggy critters onto a wagon and carted 'em outta' town." He laughed at his own cleverness.

Outside the cabin, the noise and chaos melted into peaceful quiet. Callie lay on her cot listening for any sign of the bears, but obviously they'd moved on. Never in her life had she seen such enormous animals––and so bold. Would they come back again?

A pounding on the front door jarred her upright.

"The bears have headed for the hills," a man shouted through the wall.

Charles slapped his thigh in disappointment. "Shucks," he said, "I was wishin' they'd stay the whole week; then we could skip more school."

But Callie knew better. "Even if there's no school there's still work to be done," she said, "Starting with laundry." Charles rolled his eyes at her.

"Trust me," she warned him, "By the end of the day you'll be wishing we'd had school instead." She grabbed a metal bucket and handed it to him. "Please go to the well and fill this."

While Charles was gathering water, Callie plunked the kitchen dish tub down on the floor. She tossed in a bar of laundry soap and a washboard and a ball of twine and stepped outside.

A fierce wind pelted the porch with dust. Callie fastened a length of twine between the porch posts to make a clothesline. Hopefully the thing would hold, at least for the day.

Charles returned from the well and followed her inside, water sloshing over the sides of his bucket. They hoisted it up onto the stovetop and struggled to fill the kettle.

As she lugged a basket of clothes to the porch, Callie felt a sharp twinge in her spine. Goodness, she was too young to be falling apart. Back at their farm they had a hand-cranked washing tub and wringer, which made this dreadful chore much easier. She stared at the dish tub wondering why they had to live like hobos.

Charles appeared moments later. He dutifully poured hot water from the kettle into the dish tub, then retreated into the cabin.

Callie's poor hands were already sore from the morning dishes. And by the time she'd finished scrubbing and rinsing and wringing the clothes, her skin was raw and oozing. The biting wind made her whole body ache; there was no strength left to hang these wet clothes by herself. She'd reached her limit.

"Pa! Charles!" she bellowed, "Come out here and help me!"

The door flung open as Pa and Charles clambered out. They fought against the wind, wrestling wet pieces of fabric onto the clothesline as Callie sat in a crumpled heap.

Pa's hat flew off of his head; he snatched it just before it escaped. "The way this wind's blowin'," he grumbled, "I think we're about to set sail."

Charles rubbed the grit from his eyes. "I'd rather stink somethin' awful than have to do this again," he sulked.

"I couldn't agree more," Callie said, "Why don't we just stay *dirty* from now on?"

Chapter 5: *Hopes and Dreams*

The next day at recess, the girls jumped rope as usual while the boys squatted in the dirt playing marbles.

As she turned the rope, Callie watched Miss Oliver approach the boys, accompanied by a handsome boy who looked around 16 or so. He glanced in Callie's direction and smiled, which made her feel flustered. Bertha and Martha turned their heads to see.

Callie overheard Miss Oliver's introduction. "Boys," she said, "This is our newest pupil, Billy Davis. Please make him feel welcome."

Martha shrugged. "Aw, it's just another boy," she said. "Come on, let's jump some more."

Callie turned the rope mindlessly as Martha bounced and hopped.

"I've never noticed him around here before," Bertha said in her casual way.

"Did you see his eyes?" Callie asked her dreamily, "They're the color of green grapes. And his smile..." she laughed at herself. "Heavens, I've never let myself get silly over a boy before. In fact, I used to make fun of the girls who did. Yet here I am doing the very same thing!"

"Maybe you can sit next to him Callie," Bertha teased, "That would make your heart flutter like a butterfly."

The school bell clanged and the children bounded toward the schoolhouse.

Once everyone was seated, Miss Oliver pointed to a list of math problems written on the blackboard.

"Please take out your slates and pencils and copy these problems," she said. "Solve as many of them as you can, then raise your hand when you have finished."

The classroom was hushed, except for the occasional squeak of a pencil on a slate.

Callie found herself distracted by Billy's presence. She peeked over at him, watching as he ran a hand through his thick dark hair while concentrating on a math problem.

Suddenly he looked in her direction. Callie turned back to her assignment, but her quick movement jarred the desk. Down her pencil fell, clackity-clack on the wood floor. She froze.

Billy sprang into heroic action. He jumped from his seat, swiped the stray pencil from the floor, presenting it to her like a found treasure. "Here you are," he said with a honey-warm smile.

"Th-thank you," Callie managed to reply. She turned away as her cheeks grew flushed and hot. Once Billy was seated, she peeked over again. But this time he caught her. And so did Miss Oliver.

"Callie, is there something wrong with your eyes today?" she asked. "They seem to be wandering around the room instead of focusing on the assignment."

Callie felt a sting of embarrassment. Why was Miss Oliver always picking on her? Other children did their share of clowning and speaking out of turn. One boy, Jimmy Knight, even lit a cigarette in class! Yet Miss Oliver did nothing more than ask him to snuff it out. This teacher was just plain unfair.

For the rest of the school day, Callie sat and stared straight ahead and daydreamed. In her mind she traveled back to the farmhouse, back to a place that made sense.

Finally, school let out for the day. As Callie reached the door, Miss Oliver called her.

"Callie," she said, "I know that you are a very bright girl with bright ideas. But I must keep this class running smoothly. I'm sure you understand."

Callie did not understand. In fact, she wanted to ignore the teacher and head outside, but she worried that things might get even tougher. So she stopped.

Miss Oliver motioned her closer. "I could really use some help straightening up this classroom," she said.

For the first time, Callie noticed how young Miss Oliver was––not more than 20 years old at the most. She felt almost *sorry* for her, up here in the middle of nowhere.

"All right," she agreed.

Miss Oliver smiled. "I just need some help setting up the classroom and keeping it tidy. That kind of thing."

Callie wasn't thrilled at the offer, but at least this way she stood a chance of getting on Miss Oliver's good side.

After school Callie stood in their front yard. She'd intended to start a vegetable garden, but her rake revealed nothing but rocks and more rocks. It was no use.

Charles came around the corner of the cabin with his 8 year-old school friend Lee Dolch. Lee was smart and sensitive––a good influence, Callie thought. The boys carried a bucket, a net, fishing poles, flies and lures, which flashed in the sun like tinsel.

"Where are you two headed?" Callie asked, amused at the sight of them.

"We're going fishing down at Baldwin Lake," Lee replied. "My Pa let us borrow all this stuff." The lake sat in a broad, flat valley at the edge of town. It was wide and shallow, with water the color of celery.

Callie was about to tell the boys what she'd heard about that lake, but her words were stolen by the neighbor across the road.

"There ain't no fish in there!" the man hollered from his front yard.

The three children whirled around.

"Aw, that's Jesse Walters over there." Lee said. "My Pa says you never know when Jesse's telling the truth or a big whopping lie."

Charles looked over at Jesse. "We're GOIN' FISHIN'," he said defiantly.

Callie didn't have the heart to spoil their fun. "Alright," she said, "But please be back before dusk. And catch us some supper--I'm getting awfully tired of beans."

As the boys strolled down the road, Callie watched another man stop them. Lee pointed toward the lake.

"Nope," the man said, shaking his head, "Ain't no fish in there."

The boys nodded politely, then continued down the hill, vowing not to listen to any more well-meaning souls.

The late afternoon sun dropped over the mountains. As the cabin sank into shadow, Callie thought about her brother. But just as a worry popped into her head, Charles and Lee appeared on the front porch. Their net was empty and their bucket swung lightly.

Callie put her hands on her hips. "Hmmm...where's tonight's supper?" she asked.

Charles looked downward. "Ain't no fish in there," he said. "We were fishin' in a...fishless lake."

"Oh really?" Callie replied. She noticed his body quiver with laughter.

Lee chimed in. "Yeah," he quipped, "We were two dummies standing there catching nothing but wind."

The thought of them fishing at a dead lake made Callie laugh too. "Well," she said, "I guess we're having beans again."

In the kitchen, Callie poured a can of beans into a bowl as Charles eyed her from the table. "Watch me magically turn these beans into a fish," she said, pleased at the idea.

After she mashed the beans, Callie scooped the pasty brown lump into a baking pan.

Charles watched, wide-eyed, as she squished and squeezed the lump into the shape of a trout. "Don't forget the fins," he said with a grin.

Pa got home from work in time to enjoy their surprise meal. He kicked off his boots, flung his hat onto the coat rack, and joined them at the kitchen table. As he sat down, Callie set the baking pan between them.

"What in tarnation is *this*?" Pa asked, pointing to the loaf.

Callie decided to play dumb. "Charles went fishing at Baldwin Lake today," she said sweetly.

Pa poked at the food with his fork. "Hmm. Fishin' huh?"

Charles was sure that Pa had fallen for the gag. "No no, don't listen to her," he blurted, "I didn't catch no fish. I tried to, but..."

"I know," Pa interrupted, "there ain't no fish in there. And what a shame, since it's so darn close."

Callie sensed her brother's growing frustration. She leaned forward.

"I found you a surprise out in the yard today."

His fork stopped in midair. "You *did*?"

"Yep. Finish your supper and I'll show you."

Charles shoveled his food as fast as he could. "I'm done," he said with a mouth full of beans. "Where is it?"

Callie stepped out onto the porch and returned carrying a bucket with a cloth fastened over the top. She pulled back the cloth just enough for him to peek.

"A baby lizard!" he cried. He took the bucket from Callie and carried it over to Pa and tilted it right up in his face.

"Look."

Pa scowled. "Get that thing away from me!"

Charles brought the bucket to Callie. "Can I keep it?" he asked her.

"I don't see why not. But there's one condition: if you want to have a pet, you'll have to care for it yourself."

"Sure," he said. "What do lizards eat?"

Callie winced. "They eat bugs––especially crickets. And it's your job to find them."

Charles protested, but Callie raised her hand like a warning flag.

"All right," he said, "Where can I find that many bugs?"

Callie knew there was one sure spot––a place that attracted every kind of chirping, flying, slithering, crawling creature imaginable.

"Try your luck at the well tomorrow," she said. The thought of that place at night made her shiver.

But Charles was desperate to show devotion to his new pet. He rummaged under his cot, then Pa's cot, then finally Callie's cot.

"I found a perfect house for crickets," he said, holding up his sister's round leather hatbox. He dashed out the door quick as a lightning bolt.

It was too late to stop him. Callie settled next to Pa at the table and put her head in her hands. "I'm afraid my best hat is in that box," she said.

Pa fiddled with a loose screw on his pocketknife. "Dang nabbit!" he grouched, "I use this thing at work every day. I can't have it breakin' on me."

Callie didn't know much about the stamp mill. And even though she hated the whole mining business, she was still a bit curious.

"What goes on up there all day?" she asked.

"Well," he replied, "That mill was founded two years ago in 1899 by a businessman named Captain J.R. De La Mar." Pa smiled with pride, as if he'd built the place himself.

"The gold comes outta' the mine trapped inside pieces of quartz rock. So they haul it all down to our mill. They got donkeys and mules pullin' little railroad cars fulla' gold ore––that's what they call the rock with the gold inside." He held his hands about 10 inches apart. "Big chunks like this." His eyes lit up.

Callie pictured a team of men standing around the rocks looking for crumbs of gold.

Pa stood up tall. "The ore is dropped underneath huge metal crushin' stamps." He raised his arms as if hugging a tree then let them drop, repeating the action three times.

"BOOM, BOOM, BOOM! We got 40 stamps poundin' that rock into little pieces. 130 tons of ore every day. All day and all night long."

Aha! That explained the earthquake rumbling Callie felt and heard constantly.

"What exactly do *you* do?" she asked, annoyed.

"I shovel the crushed ore into a flat bin, where we wash and sort it. Then we flush it down into the chemical vats to melt out the gold."

Callie figured Captain DeLaMar wasn't a generous man who enjoyed sharing his wealth. Tycoons rarely did; why would this one be any different?

"Do you get to keep any of the gold?" she asked, knowing full well that he didn't.

"Naw, they watch us like hawks," Pa said, pointing toward the ceiling. "Them bosses sit up there and keep an eye on us. We get paid in silver coin, though."

"It sounds like filthy work to me," Callie said, shaking her head. "And a lot harder than farm work. I'll bet you miss the farm by now, huh? I sure do."

Pa reached into his coat pocket and pulled out an envelope. "Speaking of the farm, here's a letter from Bakersfield. I'll bet it's from yer Uncle Joseph." Pa's brother Joseph was caring for the farm while Pa was here chasing this impossible golden dream.

Callie's brain stirred with excitement. "Can I see the letter, please?" she asked. "I promise I'll read it out loud." Pa slid the envelope across the table. Callie ripped it open and unfolded the heavy sheet of parchment. Uncle Joseph's handwriting was terrible, but somehow she managed to read it.

Dear James and Children,

All is well here. The alfalfa crop is growing fast, and the horses are fat and happy.

I thought you should know: Some man dressed in a fancy suit came visiting--he wanted your new address. He'll be sending you something to read over and sign. Wouldn't tell me a thing more. That's all I know. Give my regards to the children.

Yours Truly,

Joseph

Pa wiped a calloused hand over his face. "Now why would a strange fella' want our address up *here*?" he asked. "I sure hope he ain't no bill collector."

Callie had a great thought. "Let's go visit the farm! You can find out what that man wants, and we can see how everything's doing down there. It would be a nice break."

Pa dropped the letter onto the table and looked at her sympathetically. "Aw, Honey, ya know we can't just up and leave. Remember how long that wagon ride is?"

Callie scuffed over to her cot and threw herself upon it. She picked up a book and tried to read, but there was one more thing:

"Pa, do you ever stop and wonder what we're really doing up here? It's certainly all right to admit that maybe you've made a mistake."

He glared at her from the table. "You don't think I'll get rich here, do ya?"

Callie refused to lie. "Nope, I sure don't."

Charles came through the cabin door carrying Callie's hatbox.

"I've got your food, Lizzy," he said, sounding like a doting parent with a box of candy.

"*Lizzy the lizard*," Callie snipped, "That's not very original." She was still mad at him for using her hatbox as a cricket house.

As the evening wore on, those crickets chirped louder and louder. Callie slammed her book closed and sat up on her cot.

"Put those crickets out in the shed!" she said in a don't-push-me tone of voice.

Charles recognized the threat. "OK, OK. They're going out right now."

Chapter 6: *Stuff That Don't Work*

Main Street was the central gathering spot in town, with its saloon, blacksmith shop, barbershop, and general store. Callie, Charles and Pa had no choice but to visit that hostile little store every so often to stock up on necessary provisions.

One Saturday, as they left the store with sacks full of goods, they nearly tripped over a grubby group of gold prospectors sitting on the front steps. They smelled of whiskey and played homemade musical instruments and sang horribly off-key.

The storekeeper opened his door, sized up the situation, then pointed across the road.

"Why don't you boys head over to the saloon?" he half-asked, half-ordered.

A bleary-eyed prospector looked up. "They already kicked us outta there," he slurred.

"Didn't like our music, I reckon," another said. The group erupted into whoops of giddy laughter.

A small crowd of folks had gathered on the steps.

"What's the occasion?" Pa asked the bleary-eyed prospector.

The man struggled to focus his eyes on Pa. "We're celebratin' a new gold find up in Holcomb Valley," he said. The group whooped and hollered again.

The storekeeper swept a hand at them. "Naw," he said, "That claim ran dry years ago."

"Not no more it ain't," replied the prospector. "We've been dry pannin' the creek up there and it's payin' off."

Callie saw a glow wash over Pa's face. His Gold Fever was alive and well, she feared.

Pa jumped mindlessly off of the porch. Callie and Charles hurried to catch up with him as he shot like an arrow toward the barbershop.

This is an odd time for a haircut, Callie thought.

But Pa wasn't thinking about his hair. His attention was riveted on a humble-looking man fussing with a long wooden box propped on the ground. As Callie got closer she could see that the box was filled with river gravel. Beside the box sat a bucket of water and a large tin pan. The man poured the water onto the gravel.

Charles ran up to him. "Are you a prospector too?" he asked. The man removed his hat and grinned at the boy.

"Yessiree," he replied. "I'm Mr. Thomas, and I'm here to teach folks like yourself how to pan for gold the right way."

"Really?" asked Pa. "How's it done anyhow?"

Mr. Thomas clasped his hands together respectfully. "Sir, I only charge one silver coin for the lesson."

Callie couldn't believe Pa was actually falling for it.

He dug around in his pocket, then handed over a hard-earned coin.

"Gold panning is straightforward," Mr. Thomas explained as he helped Pa hold the pan. "All's you do is scoop some gravel...like this...then you dip it in the water...like this...then you shake it from side to side."

Pa tossed out a few large pieces of gravel as Mr. Thomas nodded approvingly.

"Now add a bit more water and tilt your pan to let more gravel over the side, a little bit at a time. Swirl the pan like this...Round and round and round."

"Oh Lordy," Callie groaned, "This could take forever." She looked over at Charles, who'd nearly fallen asleep standing up.

Mr. Thomas grabbed the rim of the pan. "Be careful not to tip it too far," he warned. "Now start running your fingers back and forth like this, watching for shiny specks. If one of 'em sticks to your wet finger it's probably gold."

Pa passed his hand through the murky water a dozen times. "I see lots of shiny specks but...nothin's stickin'."

"You could probably find more gold in your teeth, Pa." Callie taunted. "Shall we go?"

As they continued on their way, they came upon a small crowd gathering in front of a plump man in a black suit. He had a twisted gray mustache and wore a tall top hat. The man tipped his hat toward the Millers as they drew near, while tending to a wooden table covered with small, brightly colored bottles.

"Ladies and gentlemen," the man cried, "My name is Keller. Please gather 'round and allow me to display for you my wares: potions and remedies to heal what ails you." He nodded to Callie. "And the finest ladies toiletries available, directly from France."

Callie stepped forward for a closer look.

"You get over here," Pa ordered. "That there man's a snake oil salesman. He's sellin' stuff that don't work."

"He has oil from real snakes?" Charles asked, his mouth gaping open.

Pa shook his head and sighed. "Alright you two, we'll stay for just a bit. But we're not buyin' a thing from him--includin' any of that snake oil."

Callie stood beside the table, admiring the bottles as they shimmered like rainbows.

"Hello there, little lady," Mr. Keller said, tipping his hat again. "What can I get for you today?"

Callie picked up a bottle and struggled to read its label. "What is Laud-a-num?" she asked.

Mr. Keller looked cautiously to the left, then to the right. "Why, it's a remedy that'll stop your pain in its tracks," he whispered.

Callie thought of the pain she'd had in her heart ever since Mama died.

"I'd love to take something to stop my pain," she whispered back to him, "But...my Pa said not to buy anything from you."

"I'll tell you what," Mr. Keller replied out of the side of his mouth, "I've got one bottle here with just a bit of Laudanum; most of it spilled out. But I'll give this to you at no charge." He slipped her the bottle and she quickly tucked it into the front of her dress.

Mr. Keller gave her another wink. "I'll have more for you the next time I'm in town," he said. This was their little secret.

"Come on Callie," Pa called out, We're leavin'. Now."

They had almost reached the end of Main Street when Callie spotted Miss Oliver strolling toward them carrying a basket on one arm. She looked much prettier outside the classroom, Callie thought, hoping she appeared at least presentable.

"Good morning," Miss Oliver said with a nod.

Callie skipped over. "I have something to show you," she said. She fished the bottle from her skirt and handed it to her.

Miss Oliver's jaw dropped when she read the label. "Laudanum!" she gasped, "Why do you have this?"

"Shh!" Callie said, looking over her shoulder, "Pa doesn't know about it. That snake oil salesman over there is selling it. It's supposed to cure my pains."

Miss Oliver shook her head as she inspected the bottle. "Callie," she said, "Laudanum is a mixture of opium and alcohol. Doctors give it to patients with serious pain, but it's very dangerous."

"Can it *kill* you?"

"Yes, too much of it can easily kill you." She handed the bottle back to Callie. "When you get home, I want you to give this bottle to your father to put away. And promise me you won't take any of it--not one drop."

Callie felt an icy chill move down her spine. "I promise."

Chapter 7: *Good Medicine*

A few days later, Callie and Charles sat at the kitchen table doing their homework after school. Lizzy the lizard perched on Charles' shoulder, watching the activity in comfort.

"Algebra!" Callie complained. "What's the point of it all?" She looked up at the little reptile, envying her worry-free existence.

The front porch creaked with the sound of footsteps. Maybe Pa had gotten off work early and would help her with this horrid homework.

Suddenly the front door flew open. Two men barged their way inside, carrying a third man suspended between them.

"Pa!" Callie screamed as she recognized his face.

Charles jumped up and ran to her side with Lizzy clinging to him for dear life.

The men carried Pa to his cot and laid him on top of it as gently as they could. One of them turned toward the children.

"Your Pa hurt his arm up at the mill," he said. "We've got a nurse comin' quick. Just keep his arm still until she gets here."

Callie nodded, numb from the shock. She knelt beside the cot feeling completely helpless watching him lay on his cot moaning in pain. His arm was wrapped in a white cloth bandage.

A woman tapped lightly on the still-open cabin door, then entered.

"Hello," she called out, "This *is* the Miller residence, correct?" The woman wore a white cotton smock and a crisp nurses' cap. Slung over her shoulder was a large canvas satchel. "I'm Hannah Hopkins," she said, smiling softly.

Relief washed over Callie from head to toe. This nurse must've been sent from Heaven––perhaps by Mama herself.

Callie brought two stools from the table, offering one to Hannah and taking the other for herself. She watched as Hannah inspected the cloth on Pa's arm, then checked his forehead for fever.

"How bad is it?" Callie asked.

Hannah's voice was reassuring. "Your father will be all right," she replied, "I'm waiting for the doctor to come up from Lucerne Valley. He needs to set this broken arm."

Callie caressed Pa's forehead as he moaned and squirmed in obvious pain.

"I, I..."

"Don't try to talk, Pa. Everything will be all right."

Charles stood behind Callie, his breath heavy on her neck. He leaned over and touched the bandage, then jerked his hand back.

"I can see blood!" he cried, "It's leakin' through!"

Callie saw telltale red spots against a background of white cloth. She looked at Hannah. "How did he get hurt?"

"I couldn't get the whole story," Hannah replied, "but apparently your father's arm got too close to one of the mill's crushing stamps."

Callie cringed at the thought of Pa trapped in the jaws of that mechanical monster.

Pa struggled to raise his head. "Remember I told ya about them big stamps, Callie?"

"Shhh. Yes Pa, I remember. Please try to rest until the doctor gets here." Not knowing what else to do, Callie sat patiently for an eternity of hours.

At last there was a knock on the door. A man stepped inside, carrying a large black bag.

Hannah rose to greet him. "Hello Dr. Smith. Our patient is James Miller and these are his children, Callie and Charles."

Dr. Smith removed his hat. "My apologies for the delay," he said. "It took me four hours to get up the road from Lucerne Valley. I sure could've used one of those new horseless carriages today."

The doctor unwrapped Pa's arm and examined it carefully. Then he pulled a flask from his bag and held it up to Pa's mouth. "Mr. Miller, I'm afraid you're going to need this."

Pa took a swallow and almost choked. "Whew," he said, "That whiskey is terrible."

Dr. Smith didn't look the slightest bit amused. Well," he said, "It'll help you somewhat with the pain, but this is still going to hurt a lot." He took the flask away and dropped it into his bag. "All right, I'm going to set this fracture so that it heals properly."

He placed a piece of leather into Pa's mouth. "Now Mr. Miller, I want you to bite down on this leather so you won't break your teeth."

Callie turned away, knowing what was coming next. But Charles, with his love of nasty things, stared in awe.

Dr. Smith grabbed the arm and twisted it hard. A cracking sound filled the room, and Pa cried out through clenched teeth.

Callie couldn't help herself. She turned back to watch.

Pa whimpered like an injured puppy as Dr. Smith placed a heavy wooden cast around the arm and wrapped it tightly in a sling.

"That about does it," he said matter-of-factly, "I'll be back to examine this arm in a few weeks. Meanwhile, Hannah will come by to check on you."

After Hannah and the doctor left, Callie realized she'd forgotten about a pot simmering on the stove. Luckily she'd kept the fire burning low.

"It's a good thing we stopped at the store the other day," she said to Pa, "I'm making your favorite soup -- split pea. But unless you want me to feed you, you're going to have to eat with your left hand."

Pa sat up on his cot. "Anything for split pea," he said, gritting through his pain. He stood up and shuffled toward the table as Callie ladled out three bowls of soup.

"Charles, would you please get off your bottom and help Pa." She marveled at how lazy that boy could be at times.

As they sat down, Charles held his spoon aloft, looking first at Pa, then at Callie.

"Hannah's a real nice lady, dontcha' think?" he asked, watching their eyes. His father and sister nodded, then ate without speaking.

"I don't think she's even married," Charles continued. "At least I didn't see no ring on her finger."

No response. He cleared his throat loudly.

"I reckon she'd make someone a fine wife one day," he hinted. Finally he gave up and they finished their meal in silence.

After supper Charles helped Pa get into his nightclothes. Then Callie helped him wash his face and scrub his teeth. Together they tucked him into bed.

"I'm going to sleep like a log tonight," Callie told Charles as they readied for bed. She turned down the oil lamp; now the cabin was bathed in the faint glow of stove light.

"Aaahhhh!!!" Pa yelled at the top of his lungs.

Callie tripped her way across the room. "What is it?" she asked.

"My arm," he cried, "It's hurtin' so bad."

Poor Pa. What could she do? Her mind raced through the possibilities.

Wait, I've got just the thing for it." She lit the oil lamp and reached into the basket below her cot and pulled out a bottle. "Here. Take some of this."

Pa read the label. "Laudanum! Where in tarnation did you find this?"

She was too tired to make up a fib. "I got it from the snake oil salesman."

"Callie Rose! I thought I told you not to buy nothin' from that man." He opened the bottle and gave it a sniff. "Now don't get me wrong," he said. "I do appreciate the medicine, but I'm still gonna' punish ya' for disobeyin' me."

"But Pa, I didn't buy anything from him. He *gave* this to me."

Pa shook a few drops of Laudanum onto his tongue. "It don't matter, you shouldn't have..." And before he could finish his lecture, Pa was out like a light.

Chapter 8: *A Darn Fool*

Two weeks had passed since Pa's accident, and Callie worried that he was trying to do too much too soon. Despite the doctor's warning to take it easy, Pa had refused to sit still for more than a few minutes at a time.

On Sunday morning, Callie and Charles arrived home from church. Pa was out in the yard wearing his overalls and stirring hot coals over a pit in the ground. Smoke swirled in a gray cloud around his face.

Hannah the nurse stood in the road pleading with him to stop.

"Mr. Miller," she said, "You really need to rest that arm. The doctor plans to replace the wooden cast with a softer one, but only if it's healed enough." Pa continued to stir the coals. "*Mr. Miller,*" she repeated.

He grinned sideways at her. "Please. Call me James."

"Good morning Hannah," Callie said, shaking her head. "We can't get him to slow down either."

Hannah adjusted her heavy shoulder bag. "Well, you can't force a pig-headed man to do anything, can you?"

She said with a laugh. "I'll be back to check on him in a few days. Hopefully that arm won't fall off before then."

Charles walked over to Pa and stared at the coals. "We were all praying for your quick recovery at church," he said.

"Ya shoulda' prayed for a short sermon instead. I swear that preacher would talk 'round the clock if ya let him." He stirred the coals again. "But ya know? I think yer prayin' helped me some." He mussed the boy's hair.

As she started up the road, Hannah wagged a finger at Pa. "The praying will only help so much. You need to rest."

Pa watched her until she rounded a bend in the road. "I kinda' like that woman," he said with a smile.

Callie peered into the pit. What in the world was he cooking there?

Pa saw her puzzled expression. "I figured we'd have us a little cowboy-style barbecue," he said, lifting a long skewer of meat from the fire. "A fellow came by here this mornin' sellin' fresh beef. He had a wagon with a big block of ice in it, and the meat was layin' on top-- wrapped up and ready to go."

Charles' mouth watered in anticipation. "I want the biggest steak," he said, "'Cause I'm a hungry man."

"I'll be right back," Callie said. With newfound excitement she skipped into the cabin, returning minutes later carrying a tray with plates, utensils, and a small bowl. "I whipped together a little molasses, honey, and some black pepper," she said. "It's barbecue sauce––sort of."

Charles dragged the three kitchen stools onto the porch. "If we're eating cowboy food, let's eat outside the way they do." He then picked up a sharp stick.

"Can I roast a cricket for Lizzy?" he asked.

Pa curled his lip in disgust. "Don't even *think* about it."

After supper Callie washed the dishes, then joined Pa at the table as he sorted through the weekly mail. She leaned over his shoulder. "There's another letter from Bakersfield! Can I read it to you same as last time?"

Pa chuckled. "Well, ya' did a good job readin' yer uncle's handwriting the last time, so why not?" He handed her the thick envelope. Callie unfolded the letter, then opened her mouth to read aloud, but hesitated. This letter wasn't from Uncle Joseph after all. She scanned the signature at the bottom as Pa waited with an impatient stare. Too late, she'd have to read it now.

"Dear Mr. Miller, I am a representative of the Standard Oil Company. Our company wishes to drill for crude oil on your farmland in Bakersfield. If oil is found, we could either buy your land, or place wells in your fields. Either way, this authorization is your chance to make a large amount of money."

Callie gasped for air, then continued reading.

"If you are interested, please sign the bottom of this letter and return it immediately. Sincerely, H.M. Williams, Standard Oil Company of California."

She set the letter down and clasped a hand over her mouth.

Charles leaped for joy. "What are you gonna' tell 'em Pa?" he asked.

"I'm gonna' tell 'em to forget it," Pa replied, crumpling the letter and tossing it as if it was toilet paper.

Callie rescued the crumpled letter from the floor. "But we could have an *oil* farm! This is our chance to make free money!" she cried in disbelief. "If it was up to me, I'd bolt back to Bakersfield and sign this letter in person."

"Well it ain't up to you," Pa growled at her. "Like I told ya' before, we can't just jump down there. It ain't that easy."

Charles searched desperately for a solution. "Lee told me that most folks leave here for the winter. We could go then."

"Perfect!" Callie added, "You can sign the letter when we're home for winter break."

Pa's words cut through their enthusiasm. "We ain't goin' nowhere this winter, and that's final."

Callie was stunned by his stubbornness. Why would they have to stay here when most folks left for the winter? Didn't that dang mine ever close? She stormed out onto the porch and sat on the steps with her arms folded. "I hate gold and everything it stands for," she fumed. "Mining is the...the devil's invention!" Tears rolled down Callie's face as memories of Bakersfield flooded her head: Swimming in the Kern River on hot days; the time she fished Charles from its swift current with a stick. Picking juicy cherries in the orchard and having a contest with Charles to see who could eat more; sometimes they ate too many and had to run for the outhouse. Oh, and that one time Charles didn't make it to the outhouse and she later found his underwear in the bushes!

Then she thought of Mama's voice singing throughout the farmhouse––the voice of an angel. And now Mama was a real angel up in Heaven.

Callie got up and went back inside, fingering the choker around her neck. "I'm sorry I lost my temper, Pa," she said, patting him on the shoulder. His arm curled around her in a loving hug.

"I know, Honey-Girl," he said. "I'm just tryin' to get us a better life."

"But I thought we had a good life back home."

Pa's eyes grew misty and faraway. "All the goodness left us last year."

Callie sat on her cot, tossing the crumpled letter back and forth in her hands. "Well, we aren't gonna' find any goodness in this godforsaken town," she said.

Now it was Pa's turn to cool off. He stood up without a word and walked outside, with Charles trailing after him.

"Pa is a darn fool," Callie muttered as she uncrumpled the paper. "If he won't sign this letter from the oil company, then I will."

There was no time to waste. She tiptoed to the table, grabbed a pen, signed the letter and sealed it. Then she dashed back to her cot and shoved the letter into her school bag.

Callie felt a twinge of guilt at what she'd done. "Mama," she said, looking up to the ceiling, "I know it's wrong to deceive Pa but he just won't listen. I have to take this matter into my own hands or we'll never come home. I'm sending this letter to the oil company tomorrow."

Chapter 9: *They Ain't Savages*

The road to the schoolhouse wasn't terribly long, but on those rare days when rain fell, the usual dust turned into a muddy red clay that could suck the boots clean off your feet.

Out of necessity Callie and Charles had discovered a path through the woods with a thick carpet of pine needles that provided a firm walking surface. The pathway wound around a low hill, then conveniently dropped down onto the schoolyard.

One rainy morning they were half way along the path when Callie heard the sharp cracking of a tree branch.

"What was *that*?"

They nearly jumped out of their skin when two brown-faced children peeked their heads around a tree trunk.

"Indians!" Charles shouted.

"Shhh." Callie scolded. She knew nothing about them and she didn't want any trouble.

The native children ducked down low, but Callie could still see their shiny black hair. After a moment they picked up long sticks and started poking them high up into a pinyon pine tree. The older girl shouted instructions to the much younger boy. They used their sticks to knock pinecones to the ground.

"I wonder what they use the cones for," Charles whispered to Callie. They crept closer to get a better look.

Suddenly the native girl spun around. She spoke to the boy in a strange language, then turn back toward Callie and Charles. Slowly she raised her hand in a gesture of peace.

Callie raised her hand in return, nudging Charles to do the same. The girl then motioned them closer.

"Mu'at," she said, pointing to herself. She gestured to the shy little boy. "Ta'amit."

Callie smiled and nodded, then touched her own chest. "Callie."

Charles coughed nervously. "Me Charles," he said, sounding like his throat was full of jelly.

Mu'at held up a large cone-shaped basket filled with pine nuts. She scooped out a few of the nuts and offered them to Callie and Charles, pouring them into their hands.

"Wuh'ruh," she said, pointing toward her mouth.

Charles immediately popped the whole handful into his mouth, crunching down. Then he quickly spit them out.

Mu'at shook her head, laughing. She picked a single nut out of her palm, set it between her back teeth, gently cracked it, and pulled off the tough outer shell. Then she ate the white meat of the nut.

Charles, embarrassed by his foolishness, willingly followed Mu'at's example.

"Goodness sakes," Callie said, savoring a sweet tender nutmeat, "I didn't even know that you could eat these."

Just then, a woman's voice called out from a distant cluster of trees. The native children grabbed their basket and sticks, briefly waved goodbye, and disappeared into the woods.

"They were sure friendly," Callie said to Charles. She'd grown up hearing stories of wicked, murderous "injuns" who kidnapped children and killed off entire towns of innocent settlers. Now she wondered just how accurate these tales were. And if the attacks really did happen, perhaps they'd been provoked.

Charles nodded. "Yeah, they ain't no savages."

Callie couldn't wait to tell Miss Oliver about their encounter. "Come on Charles," she said, "I'll race you to school."

Chapter 10: *Teacher's Pet*

Class hadn't officially started, yet Callie was already at her desk facing forward and wiggling in her seat.

Miss Oliver took immediate notice. "Callie," she said, "I've never seen you so excited about school. Would you care to tell us why?" She motioned her to the front of the room.

Callie reluctantly stood there, eager to share the adventure, but afraid to speak for fear of sounding stupid. She looked over at Miss Oliver, who gave her an encouraging smile.

Surprisingly, it didn't take long for Callie to feel comfortable in front of her class. She told them all about the native children; how kind and helpful they were. And she hoped that her experience would chase away the ugly myths. Her classmates sat quietly, listening to every detail.

When Callie finished, Miss Oliver led the class in a round of applause. "Thank you," she said, "You gave a fine presentation––what a wonderful opportunity to learn about our native Serranos first-hand."

"Why are they called Serranos?" Lee asked.

Miss Oliver told the sad story of the original *Yuha-viatam* people who were enslaved by Spanish settlers and given the name Los Serranos, meaning "from the mountains". She finished the story, then glanced at the clock on the wall, shaking her head in amazement; it was already time for the recess break.

As Callie reached the door, Miss Oliver called her over to the big desk.

What have I done wrong now? She wondered.

But there was no pinch in Miss Oliver's brow.

"Callie," she said, "I see the potential for you to become a fine teacher one day. You have that special ability to connect with your audience––a quality that comes naturally and cannot be taught. Perhaps you'd be interested in being my assistant."

This came as a complete shock to Callie. She'd given up on the idea of ever impressing Miss Oliver, yet this same woman had just told her that *she* could be a teacher herself.

"Thank you ma'am," she said, feeling as if the universe had opened itself wide.

"What did Miss Oliver say?" Bertha asked as they walked over to meet Martha for hopscotch.

Callie shrugged. "I don't know why, but she asked me to be her assistant."

Bertha's face turned to stone. "Oh, that must be nice," she said.

Suddenly there was a desperate plea for help.

Callie stopped and listened. "Sounds like it's out back." The three girls followed the cries coming from behind the schoolhouse.

"Look!" Martha yelled. The outhouse had somehow tipped over and landed on its door, trapping the occupant inside.

Callie could only imagine the mess in there. "Go tell Miss Oliver," she ordered the girls, "And I'll go get the boys." It was a hilarious sight, but this was certainly not the time for giggles.

"Billy! Johnny! Charles!" she called, "Come quickly! They followed her around to the back. Billy reached the outhouse first and dropped to his hands and knees. "Are you ok in there?" he asked, with his ear to the ground.

"I th-think so," a little voice squeaked.

Charles fought the urge to laugh. "Lee! It's you!"

Miss Oliver rushed around the corner. "We'll have to raise it upright to get him out," she said. She and the boys gathered on one end of the outhouse. At the count of three, they heaved and grunted, slowly erecting the outhouse to its full height. The girls wedged rocks underneath to steady it.

Lee pushed the door open and slinked out. He waved away any further attention and sat down at the base of a tree.

Miss Oliver looked around suspiciously. "Where's Jimmy?" she asked. Everyone shrugged, except for Lee.

"Aw, Jimmy didn't mean to do it," Lee said, wiping himself with a handkerchief. "He was just trying to scare me––pretending to be an earthquake."

Miss Oliver folded her arms across her chest. "All right," she said, "Where is he?"

For a long time no one said a word. Finally Johnny dared to speak.

"Uh...Maybe Jimmy ran home." He stabbed the ground with the toe of his boot.

"Well then," she said, "I'll be sure to pay him a visit...When his father gets home."

"Teacher's pet! Teacher's pet!" Charles taunted Callie as they headed in from recess.

"Charles Miller, where did you hear such a thing?" she demanded.

He skipped along in front of her. "Bertha says you are."

It hurt her feelings that Bertha would say such a thing. "Well," she said, "I'm going to have a word with her about this."

He stopped skipping. "Please don't tell her *I* told you," he begged.

Callie waited for Bertha on the schoolhouse porch. "Bertha, you're a good friend," she said, resting a hand on her arm. "Are you mad at me about something?"

Bertha pulled a loose sliver of wood from the post. "I guess I'm a bit jealous," she whispered. "You see, I want to be a school teacher more than anything and I need to get some classroom experience. I'd planned to ask Miss Oliver if I could be her assistant, but then she offered it to you." Her lips trembled slightly.

Callie wondered why a woman was expected to be either a teacher or a nurse, and nothing else. Bertha had a perfectly good dream. But Callie's dream was so much bigger. She was determined to be an *oil farmer*.

"I'll ask Miss Oliver to make you her assistant instead of me," she said.

Bertha's eyes brightened. "You will?"

"Of course. But there's one condition."

"Anything."

"You've got to clear up your little rumor about me being teacher's pet."

Chapter 11: *Choices*

Time has a way of speeding up and slowing down, depending on the circumstances. It was now September 20th. A year ago on this same day, Mama had taken her last breath.

Callie said a little prayer in her memory, but Pa didn't seem to remember the date. Or at least he made no mention of it.

The sky was the color of dark blue velvet, and a warm breeze flowed up the hillside. This was exactly the kind of day when Mama would've itched to go trail riding. It occurred to Callie that she herself hadn't been on a horse since October; when Mama was alive she had ridden with her almost every day. Today she'd ride in her honor.

There was a particular trail that Charles and she had once explored by foot: Jacoby Gulch. This trail led to a flowing spring and had its own secret waterfall.

Callie changed into her leathers and riding boots and wide-brimmed hat, then filled a canteen. "Goodness, I can't believe it's been so long," she said to Pa.

"I'm glad yer getting' out there," Pa said, "Yer mama would want ya to."

Scout was a sturdy draft horse––a large chestnut gelding who ate twice the amount of hay as any other horse in the corral. Callie tacked him up, breathing in his sweet horsey smell, then got a leg-up from Willie, the hired stable hand. This kind-hearted man treated those animals as if they were his own.

"I do it for the love; certainly not for the money," Willie told anyone who'd listen. He was paid in gold, so it must've been true.

Callie trotted Scout through town, then headed him straight up slope to the trailhead. He moved sure-footedly up the steep rocky grade, passing between cabin-sized quartz outcroppings of yellow, red, and purplish brown. Callie felt the horse's powerful shoulders flex with each careful step, and she gave him plenty of rein, moving together as one. They crested the ridgeline, immediately free from the endless thundering of the stamp mill.

As they descended into the gulch, Callie spotted a long black timber rattlesnake stretched across the trail.

She knew that this critter was simply enjoying the warm sun, so she led Scout slightly off-trail to pass around it. But as they drew closer the snake coiled up, shaking its thick tail rattles. Scout reared up, nearly throwing Callie to the ground. She grabbed his mane tightly, leaning her body against his neck. The snake raised its head threateningly, but with one swift strike of a hoof, Scout flipped the reptile into the air, sending it into a manzanita bush. After she'd caught her breath, Callie patted Scout on the withers, then clicked him forward.

They reached the spring and Callie dismounted, leading her horse to a small clear pool where the spring flowed from the rocks. They lowered their lips to the water's surface, drinking its cool sweetness. She felt secure with her full canteen for emergency backup, as Pa had taught her.

In the distance Callie could see the soft pastel colors of the desert sweeping north and east for hundreds of miles. The land looked gentle enough to cuddle a baby, yet was as hostile as Hell; this she knew.

A wild thought popped into her head: She could escape to Bakersfield! It was straight ahead to the northwest from here. Scout knew the roads, and she had a supply of water; certainly there'd be places along the way to refill the canteen. She checked the hip pocket of her leather jacket and found two silver coins, enough to buy a few supplies. If it got too hot they could travel at night. She figured it would probably take five or six long, difficult days to get there. This was her chance—perhaps her *only* chance—to be free and go home and sleep in her own bed in a real house again.

But what about Pa? And Charles? They'd be worried sick, believing that she'd been killed by mountain lions or bears. They would search for days or weeks hoping to find any trace of her, even a few bones. And when they didn't find bones, would the townspeople blame the Indians? She wondered. They might go after Mu'at! Oh, what to do?

No answer was given, just the steady rush of wind through pines and junipers. Callie swung up into the saddle, turning her back on her dream as she headed toward the corral.

Chapter 12: *Tea and Sympathy*

A few weeks later Callie stood at the wash basin, studying her face in the mirror. Her eyelids were heavy and red and her tongue pressed against tender sores in her mouth. And what were these horrid purple spots on her arms?

"Paaaa, come take a look."

"Well I'll be darned," he said, "Ya' got the same thing I do." He staggered to a stool and sat down. "Come to think of it, I've been feelin' tired all week."

"Me too," she said, her voice shaking. "How are you feeling, Charles?"

There was no reply. Callie scanned the room until she saw Charles lying motionless on his cot and she rushed to his side.

"Charles!"

The boy moaned. His body felt limp, and was covered with the same purple spots.

"Oh Pa," Callie cried, "He's so weak. Can you summon the doctor?"

Pa shrugged helplessly. "The doctor won't be up here till next week, and Hannah ain't around neither." He rubbed his eyes. "Wait a minute! Maybe we've got that scurvy sickness. I've heard about it but never seen it for real."

"You can *die* from scurvy," Callie said, feeling a wave of panic. She'd read stories about sailors at sea who suffered slow, painful deaths from it. She knew that they carried lemons and limes on their ships to avoid the disease, but she was sure there wasn't one piece of fruit in this whole darn town. Would they die before the doctor came back?

Callie sat with her head on her knees, watching her poor brother shake from chills under a blanket. "I'm going to get some firewood from the shed," she said, struggling to pull on her boots and fighting the weakness enough to drag herself outside.

When Callie didn't return right away, Pa started to worry. He was torn between going out after her and watching over his son. Just when he was about to go searching, Callie came through the door carrying an armload of wood. She marched to the stove and stoked a roaring fire.

"I saw Mu'at out there Pa," she said. "Remember the Indian girl we told you about?"

Charles raised his head an inch off his pillow. "Right in our yard?" he asked.

Callie felt relieved to see him move, even a little. "Yeah," she said, "Mu'at came right up to me and stared at my face. She saw the spots on my skin and led me over to a pine tree and touched the branches, then lifted her hand to her mouth. She kept repeating the same thing, trying to show me something." Callie paced the floor, wishing she could figure it out.

Charles flopped his head back down, exhausted.

Suddenly there was a soft tap-tapping sound on the door. Callie opened it, but saw nobody there. As she was about to close the door she spotted a shallow, flat woven basket sitting on the porch. Inside the basket she discovered a small ceramic jug of water, along with a pouch filled with fresh pine needles.

"That's IT!" Callie cried out.

"That's *what?*" Pa asked, thoroughly confused by his daughter's behavior.

Callie set the basket on the kitchen table. "This was a gift from Mu'at," she replied. "I think she wants me to make pine needle tea."

"Pine needles for scurvy. Never heard a' that, but I guess it's worth a try."

Callie combined the needles and water in a pot on the stove. She had to have faith that this would really help them. And why wouldn't it? Mu'at's people had lived in this area for centuries; surely they knew a thing or two about survival up here.

When the tea had brewed and steeped, Callie poured a warm mugful for each of them. She held Charles' mug to his lips and prayed that this dark green liquid would be their salvation.

It wasn't until a rooster crowed that Callie realized they must've slept all day and all night. She sat up in the dim morning light and squinted over at Charles' cot. It was empty! She sprang to her feet, her eyes darting frantically.

There he was, sitting in a corner on the floor playing with toy soldiers as if nothing had ever happened.

"Mornin'," he said, his voice strong and bright. Callie ran and knelt beside him and gave him the biggest hug of his life.

"It's a miracle," she said, squishing his cheeks. "The tea really helped!" She ran to the door and flung it open, thrilled that her energy had returned.

"Thank you Mu'at," she called to the hills, "Wherever you are."

Chapter 13: *The World Changed Forever*

Though Pa didn't tell anyone, he thought of his deceased wife every single day. She'd been gone almost a year now and his heart still had a hole in it a mile deep.

But the heart can heal, just as flowers return after a hard winter. Over time, Pa had developed a fondness for Hannah. They'd struck up a little friendship––a proper one––and so he'd felt comfortable inviting Hannah to join him and the children at the Gold Mountain summer picnic. After a fine day filled with pie-eating contests, watermelon-eating contests, and gunny sack races, the four of them decided to try their hand at square dancing.

Inside the chapel, dancers whirled through the room to the sounds of fiddle music, obeying the dance caller's every command: "Forward and back! Do-si-do! Swing your partner! Promenade! Allemande left!"

Callie, Charles, Pa, and Hannah squeezed their way through the crowd. Callie saw Bertha standing with her parents and waved her over.

"It's official," Bertha said, "You and I made the best pies in the entire picnic."

"Mine looked like *cow* pies," Callie joked.

"Oh look," Bertha said, poking Callie in the ribs, "There's Billy Davis."

Callie didn't know whether Bertha liked Billy too, so she pretended not to be interested. But as soon as her friend pushed her to the front of the crowd, Callie realized there was nothing to worry about.

"Billy! Billy!" Bertha hollered across the room, "Come dance with Callie."

"I'm not going to run up and kiss him or anything," Callie said, ignoring Billy as he slowly worked his way toward them. Her face glowed like a hot red tomato; this was all too embarrassing. She smoothed her satin skirt and tightened the sash at her waist.

Charles stood beside Callie with Lizzy perched on his shoulder. But the minute he saw Lee he ran and joined him against the wall, grateful to be away from those silly girls.

"Hey Lee, guess what," he said, "I won the pie eating contest."

Lee jabbed at Charles' stomach. "It looks to me like you ate *all* of the pies."

Hannah and Pa pressed their backs into a corner, safe from stomping boots.

"Thank you for inviting me," she said, "I'm having a wonderful time."

Pa smiled so big that his cheeks hurt. "Would ya care to dance?" he asked.

"I would love to," she replied. "Let's take it easy though, because I ate too much of your roasted chicken. What a fine cook; you put me to shame."

Callie forgot all about Billy. Instead she watched as Pa led Hannah onto the dance floor, and for the first time she thought that maybe––just maybe––he was happy again.

When the music stopped, someone touched her arm gently. It was Billy.

"Will you dance with me?" he asked, flashing his light green eyes.

Callie's heart flipped and flopped. "I...I'm not much of a dancer, but...Yes I would."

Billy grinned and pointed at himself. "I don't know what I'm doing either. Let's just wing it." He took her hand and they edged out onto the floor.

Before she knew it there was Pa with Hannah, twirling right beside them. Callie immediately noticed Pa's suspicious expression and she smiled meekly.

"Pa, this is Billy Davis. Billy, this is my Pa...*Whoops!*" She stumbled.

"Nice to meet you sir," Billy said, offering a handshake.

"Mm-Hmm." Pa shook the boy's hand, then he and Hannah swirled on to the next square. As they passed by, Pa gave Callie a wink.

Callie was convinced that she and Billy were the clumsiest fools on the entire dance floor. When the dance caller shouted "Left" they turned right, and when he called "Promenade" they do-si-do'ed instead. But it didn't matter one bit; they were having the greatest time together, laughing until their bellies ached.

Eventually Callie's feet started to hurt and she felt the need for fresh air. She and Billy stood near the door catching a cool draft each time someone went in or out.

Pa and Hannah joined them, fanning their faces and necks.

"Thank you for dancing with me," Billy said, kissing Callie's gloved hand. He nodded to Pa and Hannah, then headed outside as Callie watched, sighing.

"You really like Billy, don't you?" Charles asked her without a trace of teasing.

Was it that obvious? She wondered. Well, perhaps her blushing face had given her away. Or was it the goofy smile she couldn't seem to wipe off?

"I think Billy's a right good fellow," Charles said. "And Lizzy thinks so too."

A commotion erupted in the doorway as a man entered waving a newspaper overhead. The music stopped abruptly and the dancers came to a halt, unsure of his intentions.

"He's dead!" the man hollered, "President McKinley is DEAD! It says it right here." He pointed to the newspaper headline. Gasps and cries filled the chapel.

Mrs. Metzger squeezed her way through the crowd and joined the Millers.

"It's my understanding that last week someone shot President McKinley in the stomach, but he was expected to live; isn't it a terrible shame?" She fanned herself with an empty pie tin. "I wonder how well that new President Roosevelt will handle things. After all, he's just a kid. He's even got a kid's name: *Teddy*," she huffed.

"I don't think he's old enough to shave," Pa added.

Charles looked up at Mrs. Metzger, and then at Hannah, and then at Pa.

"How could a kid be the President?" he asked with a smirk.

Mrs. Metzger suppressed a giggle. "He isn't really a *child*," she explained, "but he's only 42 years old––our youngest president ever. So in that regard, he's a youngster."

"Oh," Charles replied, still confused.

Callie tugged at the flattened fingertips of her gloves, wishing she hadn't heard the sad news. "I feel like the world has changed forever," she said. "But look at Lizzy. Everything is exactly the same for her as it was 10 minutes ago."

"She's a simple critter all right," Charles acknowledged.

At that moment Callie wished that their lives could be that simple too.

Chapter 14: *One Big Broken Dream*

Times were changing in Gold Mountain, and most definitely for the worse. Not only was the gold harder to find, but outlaws seemed to be running the whole town. Gunshots rang out nearly every night and rough characters perched along Main Street like hungry vultures.

These days Miss Oliver walked the children to school, accompanied by a neighbor man toting a rifle. And during recess she sat on the porch watching over them the way a shepherd tends her flock.

"This town is in trouble," Callie said as she turned the jump rope.

Martha bobbed her head. "My mama won't let me play outside by myself anymore."

"I don't know what we're going to do," Bertha moaned, "My father is the postmaster, and I'm terrified that someone's going to rob him or...Oh, I can't even think about it."

A sharp *Whack!* sound came from the other end of the school yard. The girls spun around to look.

"What are you doing?" Callie yelled.

"We're playin' golf," Charles yelled back. He and the other boys gripped heavy sticks. Charles swung his stick and *Whack!* hit a round rock straight into a gopher hole.

Jimmy waved his stick in the air. "I'm gonna' keep this," he said. "Yesterday three outlaws robbed the assay office and killed the assayer. Two of 'em rode off, but one was cornered by some of our men––they trampled the scalawag with their horses."

This got Charles' attention. "Is he dead?" he asked excitedly. "Can we go see the body?"

"Naw, he's tied up in the back of the saloon I hear," Jimmy said, "but he deserves to die, if you ask me."

Miss Oliver rang the bell and gathered the children onto the schoolhouse porch.

"All right," she said, "Things have been difficult for everyone lately, so I'm happy to have some good news: A new sheriff is coming to town to restore law and order."

"Will the sheriff run the dang outlaws out of here?" Lee asked.

She nodded. "Those men are cowards, plain and simple. They see a town in trouble and they take advantage of it. But once word gets out about the sheriff, they'll go somewhere else."

"Usually they take the outlaws up to the hanging tree," Johnny said.

Callie had heard about that tree. It was a tall juniper on a hillside. Charles tried many times to show her the place where, supposedly, more than 25 men had met their deaths.

Miss Oliver clicked her tongue. "Hanging is against the law nowadays," she said. "They should let the sheriff arrest the man and take him to San Bernardino."

"They don't wait for no law up here," Jimmy sneered.

"We live in a civilized country governed by laws," she countered. "If they hang him without a proper trial, then...they're guilty of a crime too. It's unacceptable."

Johnny nodded in agreement. "I know ma'am," he said, "But I don't think there's any way we can stop them."

For a moment, Callie thought she might be going deaf, straining to hear a sound that suddenly wasn't there. What in the world could it be?

Silence. A silence more deafening than the night-and-day background rumbling she'd long ago become used to.

"The stamp mill!" she cried, "It stopped."

The class stirred anxiously as Miss Oliver opened the door and peered outside.

"They're coming this way," she said, dismayed. "The workers––all of them, I think." She put a hand over her forehead and sunk into her chair.

The men grew closer, grumbling and cursing loudly. Callie heard Pa's voice the loudest as they passed the open doorway.

"Ya know what chaps my hide," Pa said to the others, "They didn't give us no warnin'. Just shooed us outta' there like we were flies."

"Yep," another agreed, "They worked us to death, squeezed every drop out of us, then dumped us out for slaughter. Just like old milking cows."

Jimmy popped up from his seat. "Is my Pa gonna' pull me out of school now?"

Miss Oliver stood up with a renewed sense of pride. "Absolutely not!" she insisted. "The school year is almost over; you all have the right to finish. No other decisions will be made till then."

That evening Pa attended an urgent town hall meeting in the chapel. Back at the cabin, Charles played with Lizzy on the porch while Callie sat at the kitchen table cleaning out her school bag. As she pushed the clutter into a pile she spied an open letter on the table. She figured it wasn't private, or Pa wouldn't have left it sitting out.

Dear Mr. Miller,

We received your authorization for crude oil exploration on your property. As stated in our original offer, if a reliable source of oil is discovered in the first test well, Standard Oil Company will pay you a royalty based on every barrel of crude removed thereafter.

We may also offer to purchase your property outright, depending on our mutual interests. We look forward to a profitable relationship with you.

Sincerely,
H.M. Williams,
Standard Oil Company of California

Callie's heart bounced around her ribcage. She jumped to her feet, confident that the oil company would indeed find plenty of oil from the moment they started digging. She held the letter overhead like a trophy, twirling round and round till she nearly dropped from dizziness. Then she flopped onto her cot and stared at the ceiling. "Mama!" she cried, "I did the right thing after all. We're one step closer to going home––I can *feel* it!"

Chapter 15: *Opportunity*

Pa's decision to leave Gold Mountain City was swift. As his children were finishing their last school day and completing their final examinations, he loaded crate after crate of belongings onto the wagon, packing only the most important necessities.

The following morning the family invited Hannah for a farewell breakfast. Their kitchen table sat out on the porch surrounded by three stools and an upside down crate. Hannah arrived carrying a basket of hot biscuits, and Pa stepped from the porch to greet her.

"Mighty glad ya could join us on such short notice," he said.

Hannah looked at him sharply. "I couldn't miss a chance to say goodbye."

"I'm glad that *someone* here will miss us," he said, grinning slightly.

Callie came out through the door carrying two large bowls. "Well, I've used up the entire pantry; I sure hope you're all hungry." Then she noticed the basket of biscuits; there was no way they'd finish all of this food. Oh well.

Pa heaped a mound of beans onto his plate. "The new sheriff is still tryin' to find out who hanged that outlaw," he said. "And of course no one's sayin' a thing".

Hannah frowned. "I'm afraid this town doesn't have much of a future."

Pa nodded. "Yep, and that's why Callie decided we'd best pack up and get outta' here."

"*You* decided?" Hannah asked, wide-eyed.

Callie stopped eating and stared at a chip on the edge of her plate.

"I forgot tell ya about that," Pa said. "Awhile back, Callie signed a letter––she was pretendin' to be me. The letter she signed gave some big oil company permission to drill on our farm land."

Charles dropped his fork. "Huh?"

Hannah dabbed her mouth with a napkin. "James, that's wonderful! How lucky you are to have such a fine opportunity."

"Well I reckon we'll soon find out." He gave Callie a wink.

"You aren't mad at me Pa?" she asked, amazed that he hadn't tanned her hide.

He tugged on one of her braids. "Sometimes I think ya got a whole lot more sense than I do. This town is one big broken dream, and you saw it long before I did. But it's never too late; we've still got our dreams, ain't that right?"

Callie saw a pang of sadness as he smiled at Hannah.

"Ain't no future for ya here I suppose," he said. "Ya fixin' to move on somewhere?"

"And leave all this?" she asked, laughing. "Actually I've got job offers from two hospitals: one's in San Bernardino and the other is in Bakersfield––isn't that a strange coincidence?"

Pa took a long breath and exhaled hard. "When will you know which place you're goin' to?"

Hannah looked at him playfully. "Oh, I've already decided that I'd much rather go to..."

"To where?" he asked.

"To..."

"Where, dang it!" he demanded.

Hannah's eyes lingered for a moment longer. "Why, *Bakersfield* of course."

Callie bristled with excitement. She hoped that it was true; that Hannah would soon join them and see their farm. She pictured the four of them together, laughing and holding hands like a family. And she was absolutely sure that Mama wouldn't mind it one bit.

Hannah stood up from the table. "Well, I should excuse myself so you can finish packing." She pulled the brim of her bonnet low on her face, but Callie could still see tears welling in her eyes as they walked her to the road.

"See you in Bakersfield," Hannah called, as a breeze whipped the folds of her skirt. And then she was gone.

Miss Oliver, Billy, and Bertha stopped by to say their farewells.

Callie's eyes met Billy's. "Congratulations, graduate!" she beamed. "So, where are you headed to now?"

Billy adjusted his suspenders. "Jimmy Knight's family has a springtime job for me at their lodge on Big Bear Lake," he said, "And *that* lake actually has fish in it!" He winked at Charles.

Callie didn't want to lose track of Billy if she could help it; this required boldness.

"Maybe you could come visit us on the farm this winter," she offered. "*Millers' Acres*, we call it."

Billy grinned wider than the Grand Canyon. "I'd like that very much," he said, kissing her hand.

Pa grunted his approval.

"And what about you Bertha?" Callie asked.

Bertha's face drooped with dread. "We're staying," she said. "My family's been mining up here for years. If

Gold Mountain runs dry we'll just find another one; there are plenty of mines in these hills." As the two girls hugged, Callie made a silent wish for her friend that she'd one day achieve her dream of teaching school.

Miss Oliver cocked her head slightly as Callie came closer.

"So this is goodbye," she said, heaving a sigh.

Callie thought back over these past months of school, remembering the way she'd resented Miss Oliver in the beginning. It was funny just how much this teacher had changed over time––or was it *she herself* who had really changed? Callie wasn't quite sure. Either way, now they were about to part company.

"Are you planning to stay up here?" she asked Miss Oliver.

"I'll stay till the school runs out of children," she replied with a laugh. "But I sure will miss you and Charles."

Callie took Miss Oliver's hands in hers. "Thank you," she said, "For everything."

As soon as the well wishers had left, Pa headed straight for the porch. He tossed the empty bowls and plates from the table into the cabin, then closed the front door.

"Well," he said, brushing off his hands, "I guess we're ready to roll."

"What happens to all the stuff that we ain't takin'?" Charles asked.

Pa shrugged. "It was sittin' there when we got here. We'll just leave it for the next folks––poor suckers."

Callie pointed to the wagon. "The only thing I have to take is Mama's trunk."

Charles picked up Lizzy's bucket. "And this is all I'm takin'," he said.

Pa propped his foot on the spoke of a wagon wheel. "Ya know Son, that lizard would have a tough time on the road. Ya oughtta' just let her go."

Charles lifted Lizzy from her bucket, holding her like a baby. "No! I can't turn her loose like that––she's my friend."

Callie stroked Lizzy's smooth cold skin. "She's still a wild animal Charles, and we took her out of her natural home. Maybe she has a family; maybe she misses her lizard friends." They laughed at the thought.

"OK," he said. "Where should we put her?"

"We found her in this yard, so why not right here?"

Charles bent low and gently set Lizzy on the ground. "Be free," he said. But the critter didn't move. "See!" he cried, "She ain't runnin' off. She wants to go with us."

Callie surrendered. "If she wants to go, then she goes."

Charles scooped Lizzy up and kissed her pointed nose.

"Awright," Pa said as he climbed onto the wagon, "All aboard for Bakersfield." He pulled an envelope from his jacket pocket. "We just got one stop at the post office on the way outta'town. I'm lettin' yer Uncle Joseph know that we're on our way."

Callie grasped the locket on her choker and looked up at the sky. "We're coming home, Mama," she said, "Please help us get there safely."

Chapter 16: *Full Circle*

After six days of cold and dust and misery, they reached the wide flat Central Valley.

"I can see Bakersfield from here," Callie cried, standing in her seat and rubbing her sore bottom.

Two hours later they pulled onto the familiar long driveway. Uncle Joseph rode out to meet them as the dogs barreled after him and barked their greetings. He pulled his horse alongside the wagon.

"Welcome!" he hollered over the barking. "You've arrived none too soon."

Callie was thrilled to see that everything looked exactly the same as they'd left it.

"How was your ride through the Tehachapi Pass?" asked Uncle Joseph.

Charles' face brightened. "We saw lots of wagons that broke down. And one of 'em even went over a cliff."

He shook his head. "Well, that's all behind you now. Take a look over here. This way." They followed him past the house and back by the barn.

"Look!" He pointed between the structures.

Pa halted the wagon and gasped.

There in the middle of an alfalfa field stood a towering oil well.

"Dang!" Pa said. "And to think that this was under our feet the whole time!"

"Yep," Uncle Joseph replied. "It's a real gusher too. Like Niagara Falls."

Mama would be so happy for us all, Callie thought, fighting tears.

"Can we get closer to it?" Charles asked.

"Tomorrow," Pa said, dazed.

After supper and a long hot bath, Callie sprawled out on her girly pink bed surrounded by white painted furniture and frilly curtains. Although she preferred this way of life, she now knew that she could live just about anywhere——including a rickety one-room miner's cabin.

She thought back over the past year, convinced that Pa's search for treasure had been a quest for something he'd lost when Mama died.

Well, Mama's spirit had never really left them and as it turned out, the treasure was right in their own back-yard. They'd traveled in a big circle like a cat chasing its tail, ending up in the same place they started. The whole time, Pa never found one flake of that shiny yellow metal. But he sure struck gold anyhow. *Black* gold.

And even though she'd missed home terribly, Callie learned something from her family's journey: As long as they had each other, they had everything they needed.

EPILOGUE

Although Callie, Pa, and Charles Miller are fictional characters, the town of Gold Mountain was a real place with a very short history. It was originally established as "Bairdstown" in 1874 to accommodate the needs of workers at the nearby Gold Mountain (or Lucky Baldwin) Mine and stamp mill, named for E.J. "Lucky" Baldwin. After the Baldwin mill burned down in 1878, a new mill was built in 1900 by J.R. DeLaMar. Bairdstown was renamed "Gold Mountain City". Oddly, the town was also called "Doble", named for Budd Doble, Baldwin's son-in-law. In 1901 the schoolhouse was opened, with the real Miss Margaret Oliver as its first teacher.

Because of the up-and-down nature of mining in the area, the population began to dwindle after 1902. The school closed in 1909, and Gold Mountain/Doble soon became a ghost town. The Gold Mountain Mine remained active, but it was never prosperous. After a series of starts and stops, it was all but abandoned. By

1923, the stamp mill was silenced forever. Small mining claims continued to work the area, producing limited yields of gold ore.

Meanwhile, across Bear Valley the neighboring town of Pine Knot (now Big Bear Lake, California) was growing steadily. With a large man-made lake, Pine Knot attracted seasonal visitors to vacation along its picturesque shores. The lake was also referred to as "Bear Lake". Historians disagree as to when it officially became known as Big Bear Lake.

At the same time, the area surrounding Bakersfield was booming with the discovery of large crude oil reserves. Farmers were indeed becoming millionaires—almost overnight. Interestingly, large deposits of crude oil still exist there, and continue to be productive to this day.

As for the gold, well, it waits to be unearthed up in the San Bernardino Mountains. However, over many decades it has proven too difficult to justify the expense of mining it. Perhaps it is simply the fate of this golden treasure to remain hidden in these mountains forever.

LIVING HISTORY

If you would like to learn more about the diverse and fascinating historical past of California's Big Bear/San Bernardino mountain regions, please visit the Big Bear Historical Museum. The Museum is operated by the non-profit *Big Bear Valley Historical Society*, which is dedicated to preserving the area's rich past, present, and future:

Big Bear Valley Historical Society
P.O. Box 513
Big Bear City, CA 92314
Tel: (909) 585-8100
Web site: http://www.BigBearHistory.org

(All images in this book reprinted with permission of the Big Bear Valley Historical Society)

FURTHER READING

Abbott, E.E. et al. (1990). "Big Bear Yesterday", Redlands Federal Savings & Loan Association, Redlands, CA

Bellamy, S.E. & Keller, R.L. (2006). "Images of America: Big Bear", Arcadia Publishing, Charleston, SC

Big Bear Valley Historical Society/Big Bear Museum (perpetual collections). Big Bear City, CA

Cornett, J.W. (2002). "How Indians Used Desert Plants", Nature Trails Press, Palm Springs, CA

Core, T.H. (1993). "Ghost Town Schoolmarm". The Core Trust, Big Bear City, CA

Fincher-Reichardt, B. and Brown, R. (1983). "The Indians of Big Bear Valley", Big Bear Valley Historical Society, Big Bear City, CA

Gregory, K. (200)1. "Seeds of Hope: The Gold Rush Diary of Susanna Fairchild", Scholastic, Inc., New York, NY

Johnston, F.J. (1973). "The Serrano Indians of Southern California", Malki Museum Press, Morongo Reservation, Banning, CA

Kalman, B. (1999). "The Gold Rush (Life in the Old West", Crabtree Publishing Co., New York, NY

Keppler, R. (2003). "Vanishing Big Bear", Fifty Three/Fifty Publications, Big Bear City, CA

Murphy, C.R. & Haigh, J.G.(2001). "Children of the Gold Rush", Alaska Northwest Books, Portland, OR

[From World Wide Web]. (2007).Four Directions Inst., URL: http://www.fourdir.org/serrano.htm